IF ALL THE SEAS WERE ONE SEA;
JUVENILE FICTION DOM J 1

D0941034

DATE DUE

| NO 4 '94 | | | |
|---|---|---|---|
| | | | |
| | | | |
| MR 15 '96 | | | |
| 6 '98 | | | |
| | | | |
| | | | |
| | | | |
| | | | |

DEMCO 25-380

RIVERSIDE CITY COLLEGE
LIBRARY
Riverside, California

DEMCO-FRESNO

# IF ALL THE SEAS WERE ONE SEA

ETCHINGS BY JANINA DOMANSKA

THE MACMILLAN COMPANY, NEW YORK

COLLIER-MACMILLAN LTD., LONDON

Riverside Community College
Library
4800 Magnolia Avenue
Riverside, California 92506

PZ8.3.D698 If 1971
Domanska, Janina.
If all the seas were one
sea;

Copyright © Janina Domanska 1971

All rights reserved. No part of this book may be reproduced or
transmitted in any form or by any means, electronic or mechanical,
including photocopying, recording or by any information storage and
retrieval system, without permission in writing from the Publisher.

The Macmillan Company, 866 Third Avenue, New York, N.Y. 10022
Collier-Macmillan Canada Ltd., Toronto, Ontario
Library of Congress catalog card number: 73-146621
Printed in the United States of America

2  3  4  5  6  7  8  9  10

The art was prepared in four colors—etchings on zinc plates for
blue and black and brush-and-ink overlays for red and green.
The typeface is Weiss roman, with display lettering etched by the artist.

TO SUSAN WITH LOVE

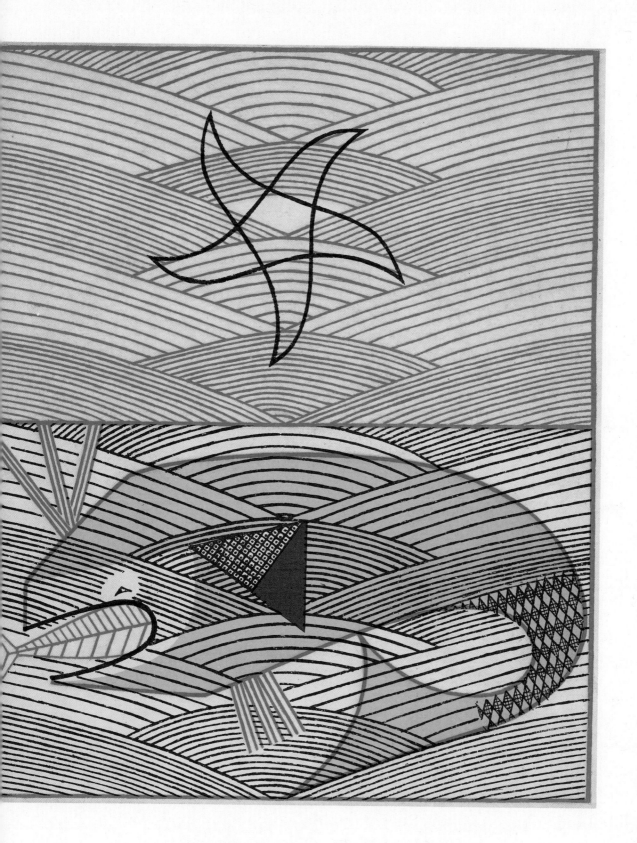

If all the seas were one sea,

what a great sea that would be.

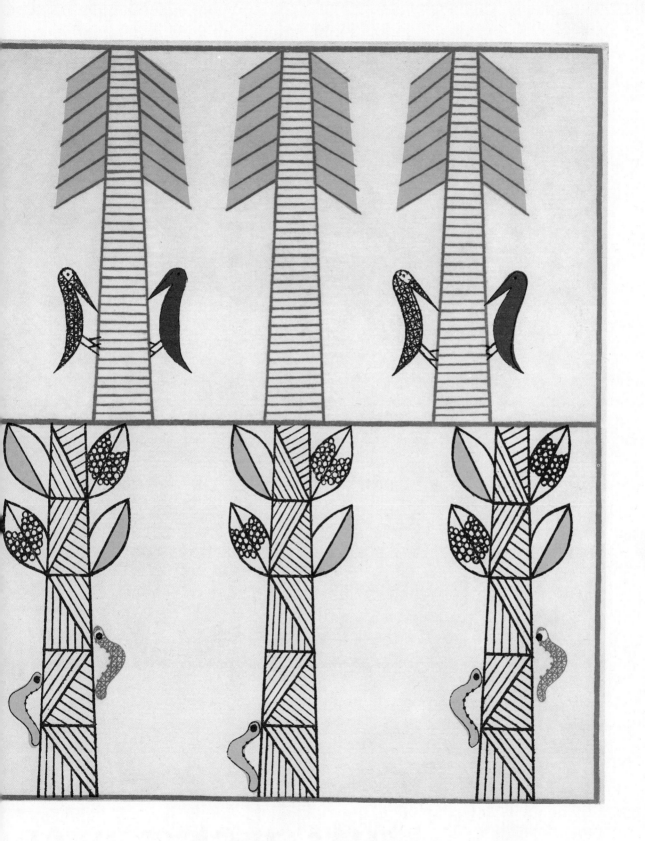

And if all the trees were one tree,

what a great tree that would be.

And if all the axes were one ax,

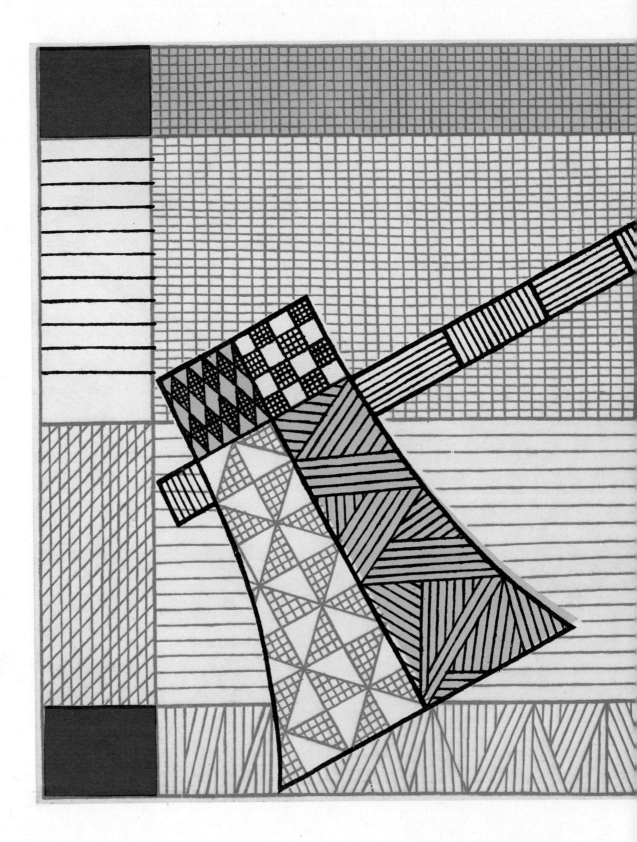

what a great ax that would be.

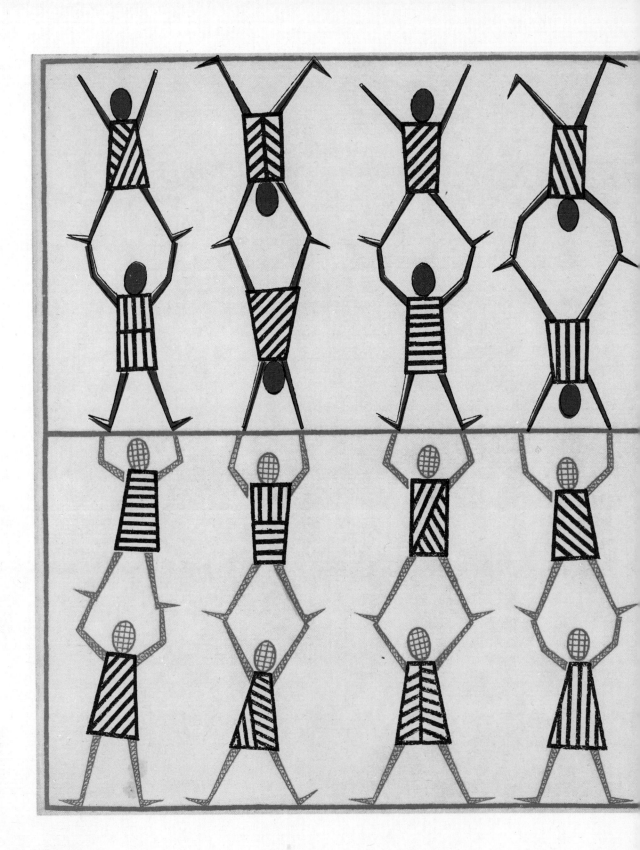

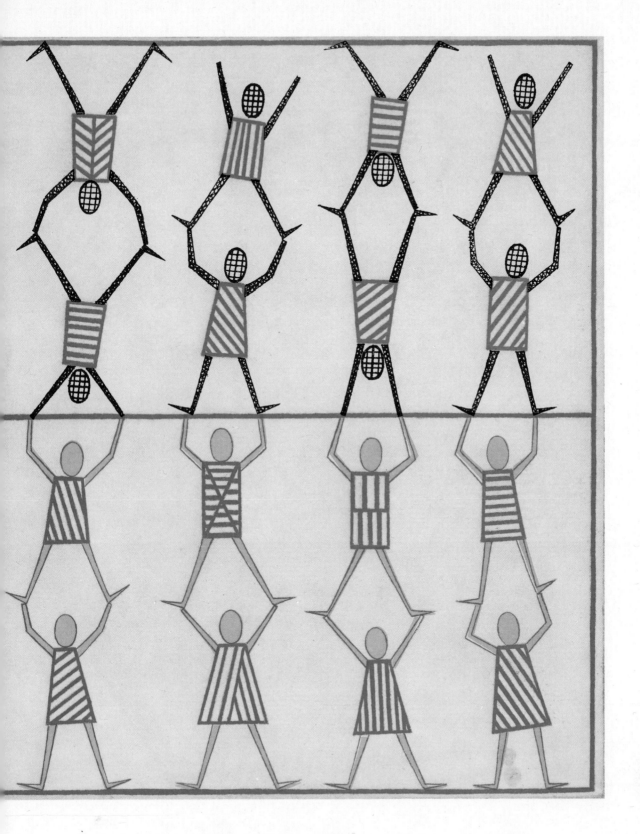

And if all the men were one man,

what a great man that would be.

And if the great man

took the great ax

and cut down the great tree

and let it fall

into the great sea,

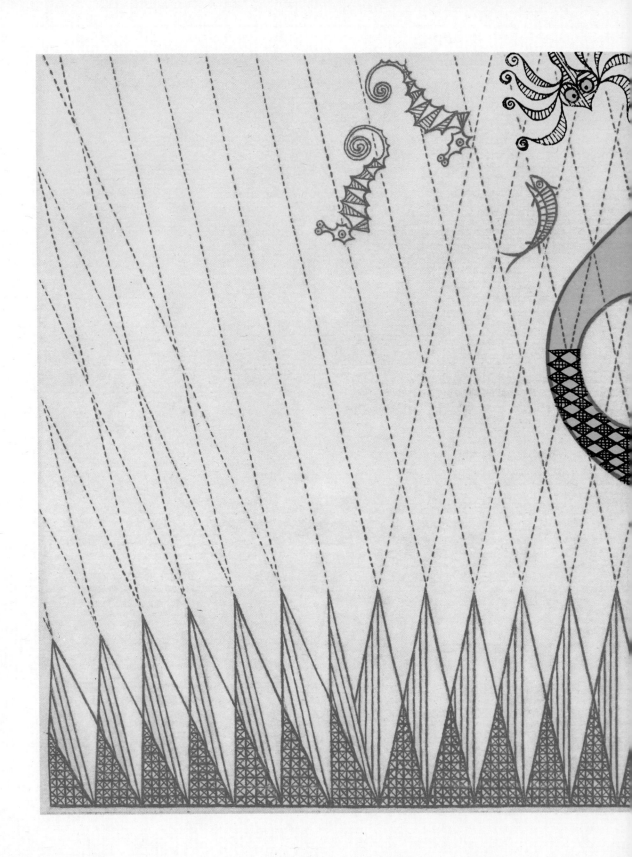

what a splish splash that would be!